Little Stories Series

- A BOOK ABOUT FRIENDSHIP -

Elephant
and
Queen Bee

Fleurie Leclercq

Illustrated by Eli Om

THIS BOOK BELONGS TO:

_____

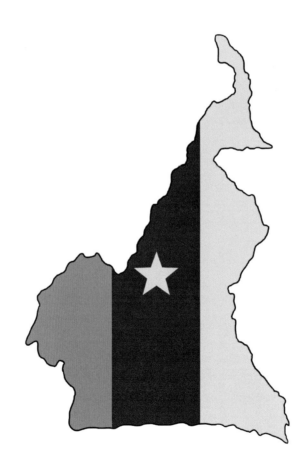

Cameroon, The Majestic Little Africa

Elephant and Queen Bee

ISBN: 979-8-507303-39-7 (Paperback) | ISBN: 978-1-949757-25-5 (Hardcover)

First Printing 2021

NDE MEDIA GROUP
NOBILITY. DIGNITY. ELEGANCE.
www.snowflowerbooks.com

For my children - Jules, Louis and Marguerite.

And for the world. I pray for all living beings to be free, for all living beings to be happy, for all living beings to find their existential purpose, and for all living beings to realize their sublime nature.

"
In the beginning was the Word,
and the Word was with God,
and the Word was God.

– John 1:1
"

Elephant was very happy.

She had a lot of friends and lived under a great big banyan tree. She loved the tree because the leaves gave her shade from the hot sun, allowing her to relax.

8

A hive of bees, led by their queen, shared the tree with Elephant.

The bees were very busy creatures and were always making honey.

They loved the banyan tree because it gave them so many nearby flowers for nectar.

Unfortunately, the Queen Bee and Elephant did not get along. Elephant did not like how the bees buzzed all the time, even when she was napping. She thought they were so annoying!

16

Queen Bee also did not like Elephant. Elephant was always sleeping on the bee's flowers.

She thought Elephant was so lazy!

Then, one night, there
was a terrible storm.
Lightning flashed.

18

Thunder crashed. Angry wind shook the entire banyan tree from trunk to branch to leaf.

When morning came, the banyan tree was a mess.
The leaves were everywhere but on the tree.
The branches had snapped and fallen to the ground.

Queen Bee no longer had a branch for her hive,
and Elephant no longer had shade.

22

Elephant shouted at Queen Bee. "My home is ruined! Would you tell your bees to stop buzzing about? They're annoying me!"

24

"My home is ruined, too!"
said Queen Bee.

"Would you stop stomping
on our flowers?"

Elephant tried to put the leaves back on the tree, but they wouldn't stay.

27

Queen Bee tried to get her workers to put the hive back, but it was too heavy. Elephant saw what Queen Bee was doing, and Queen Bee saw what Elephant was doing.

They thought for a moment...

"We both need help," said Elephant. "No use in arguing. Let me help you put your hive back in the tree." Queen Bee nodded.

"My workers and I can gather the leaves and attach them back to the tree using our sticky honey!"

Elephant and Queen Bee, once rivals, worked together to make their home a nicer place. They realized they both had value, and if they worked together, their lives would be better.

Elephant promised not to sit on the flowers and the Bees kept their buzzing down when Elephant was trying to nap. They became the best of friends.

They learned that we can do so much better when we are together.

The End

Why are bees important? And how you can help them?

1

Bees are in decline due to pesticides, habitat loss and climate change.

2

But they are essential to biodiversity!

3

Many fruits, flowers, and plants reproduce through bees pollination.

4

Humans and animals depend on them for food!

5
Bee the Solution!

* Bee respectful
* Do not use pesticides
* Plant bee-friendly flowers
* Support local hives
* Spread awareness
* Get your own hive

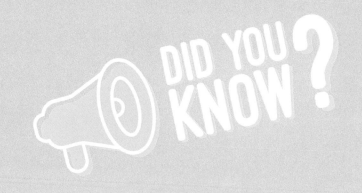

Elephants are the **largest land animal**
But they are afraid of **bees!**

DID YOU KNOW?

Elephants are the only mammals that cannot **jump, trot, or gallop.** But they know how to **swim!**

DID YOU KNOW?

Elephants eat so much!
They spend up to three-quarters
of their day just **eating!**

Elephant and Queen Bee

Bees and Elephant
Do not get along
Will they find a way
Once their home is gone?

With each other's help
They could save their tree
Listen to Elephant
and Queen Bee

Little Stories
Little Stories
The world is full of hope
Little Stories
Little Stories
Will make you wise and strong

No need to argue
No need to reject
Here's a simple truth:
No one is perfect

Working together
Gathering our strenghts
Is the smartest way
to make new friends

Little Stories
Little Stories
The world is full of hope
Little Stories
Little Stories
Will make you wise and strong

Books Mission Statement

Snow Flower Books was founded by Fleurie Leclercq, who grew up in the village of Yaounde in Cameroon, Africa. She wrote her first book, *Snow Flower and the Panther*, in order to showcase her African culture through the eyes of a young girl living day by day with pride in her heritage and community. Fleurie's stories explore what it means to grow up with a true village mentality: understanding the value of togetherness, kind-ness, and sharing your purpose with those around you.

Snow Flower Books envisions a future full of self-expression, unconditional love, and balance between people and the planet. Join us on our mission to empower children of all backgrounds to discover their inner-light and share it with the world in order to make it a more kind and beautiful place. And remember: it takes a village; so spread the love.

OTHER BOOKS BY FLEURIE LECLERCQ

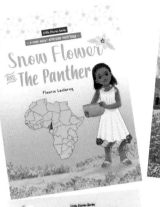

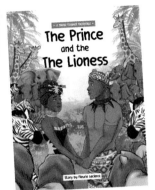

Also available in SPANISH and FRENCH!

Check out our best selling series at
www.snowflowerbooks.com

Available on Amazon.com

Made in the USA
Middletown, DE
18 April 2023

28978390R00029